Dr. Brad Has Gone Mad!

Dr. Brad Has Gone Mad!

Pictures by
Jim Paillot

Dan Gutman

HARPER

An Imprint of HarperCollinsPublishers

To Emma

Library of Congress Cataloging-in-Publication Data

Gutman, Dan.

Dr. Brad has gone mad! / Dan Gutman ; pictures by Jim Paillot. — 1st ed.

p. cm. — (My weird school daze ; #7)

Summary: Ella Mentry School counselor Dr. Brad believes wisecracking A.J. may be a genius and subjects him to some very weird tests to find out for sure.

ISBN 978-0-06-155414-8 (lib. bdg.) — ISBN 978-0-06-155412-4 (pbk.)

[1. Schools–Fiction. 2. Counselors–Fiction. 3. Psychological tests–Fiction. 4. Humorous stories.] I. Paillot, Jim, ill. II. Title. III. Title: Doctor Brad has gone mad!

PZ7.G9846Dq 2009   2009014566

[Fic]–dc22   CIP

                                                                         AC

Typography by Joel Tippie
09 10 11 12 13   CG/RRDB   10 9 8 7 6 5 4 3 2 1
❖
First Edition

Contents

Little Miss Perfect

My name is A.J. and I hate school.

It was Monday morning. I had just walked into Mr. Granite's third-grade class. Everybody was putting stuff into their cubbies. My friends Ryan and Michael were talking about a football game they watched over the weekend.

Andrea Young, this annoying girl with curly brown hair, was talking with her friend Emily about jewelry.

"Do you like my new necklace?" Andrea asked Emily. "It says 'LOVE' on the back."

"It's really shiny," Emily said, "and it goes so nicely with your skirt."

"I love to accessorize!" Andrea said.

Ugh. Girls are so annoying. I didn't even know what "accessorize" meant, but it was obviously some girly thing that girls do.

"G'day, mates!" said Mr. Granite. "Take out your reading log."

Reading log?

I don't have a reading log. Who wants to read a log? How would you write on a log,

anyway? I guess you'd have to carve into it with a knife. But how would I carry a log to school? My backpack is heavy enough without having to put a log in there.

"I don't have a—" I started to say.

"He means your notebook, dumbhead," Andrea whispered to me, rolling her eyes.

"I knew that," I lied.

The Human Homework Machine thinks she is *sooooooo* smart. Me and the guys call her Little Miss Perfect. For fun, Andrea reads the dictionary.

What is her problem? Why can't a reading log fall on her head?

Actually, I didn't have to take out my reading log after all. Because at that moment, the most amazing thing in the history of the world happened. There was a knock on the door.

Well, that's not the amazing part, because doors get knocked on all the time. The amazing part was what happened next.

"A.J.," Mr. Granite said, "will you please answer the door?"

"How can I answer the door?" I asked. "Doors don't talk."

"*I'll* do it," said Andrea, rolling her eyes again.

Little Miss Perfect opened the door. The school secretary, Mrs. Patty, was standing there.

"Mr. Granite," she said, "will you please send A.J. to Mr. Klutz's office?"

"Ooooooooooooooooooooooooh!" everybody ooooooohed.

"A.J.'s in *trouble*!" said Michael, who never ties his shoes.

"What did you do *this* time, A.J.?" asked Ryan, who will eat anything, even stuff that isn't food.

"Did you rob a bank?" asked Neil, who

we call the nude kid even though he wears clothes.

"Maybe you'll finally get kicked out of school, Arlo," said Andrea, rubbing her hands together.*

Andrea calls me by my real name because she knows I don't like it.

"Your *face* should get kicked out of school," I told her.

I thought about all the bad things I had done recently. Maybe it was the time I put a worm in Emily's sneaker during recess. Maybe it was the time I wrote KICK ME on a piece of paper and taped it to Andrea's

---

*When people want something really bad, they rub their hands together. Nobody knows why.

7

back when she wasn't paying attention. I must have done something really horrible to be sent to Mr. Klutz's office.

Bummer in the summer! I wanted to run away to Antarctica and go live with the penguins. Penguins are cool. They never get sent to the principal's office.

I walked really slowly down the hall. The slower you walk, the longer it takes to get anywhere. If you walk slow enough, by the time you get to the principal's office, he might forget the bad thing that you did. So always walk to the principal's office *really* slowly. That's the first rule of being a kid.

Finally, after about a million hundred

hours, I reached Mr. Klutz's office.

I put my hand on the doorknob.

I turned the doorknob.

I pulled open the door.

And you'll never believe the amazing thing I saw in there.

I'm not gonna tell you what it was.

Okay, okay, I'll tell you. But you have to read the next chapter first. So nah-nah-nah boo-boo on you!

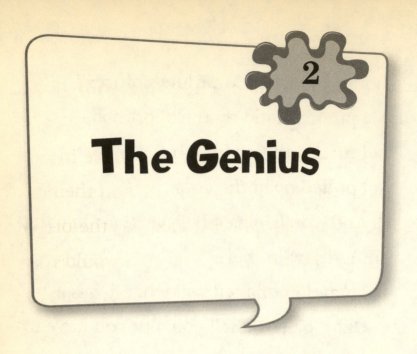

The Genius

I knew you'd keep reading!

When I opened the door to Mr. Klutz's office, Mr. Klutz was in there. Well, duh! Who else would be in Mr. Klutz's office?

But that's not the amazing part. The amazing part is what Mr. Klutz was doing in his office.

He was playing Ping-Pong with himself!

Mr. Klutz had a Ping-Pong table in his office. He would hit the ball, and then he would run around the table to the other side and hit it back. Then he would run around the table and hit it back again to himself.

Mr. Klutz is nuts.

"Hello A.J.!" Mr. Klutz said when he noticed I was standing there. "Ping-Pong is great for getting rid of stress. Have a seat."

"Where did you get a Ping-Pong table?" I asked.

"From Rent-A-Ping-Pong-Table," Mr.

Klutz replied. "You can rent anything."

Mr. Klutz was all out of breath from running around the Ping-Pong table. He sat down and asked me about the weather and what I ate for breakfast and other stuff that nobody would ever care about. Principals always make chitchat before they tell you the horrible thing that you did. Nobody knows why.

There was a knock on the door, and Ms. Coco came in. She's in charge of the gifted and talented program at Ella Mentry School. I didn't want to be in the G and T program, but she forced me. Ms. Coco made some chitchat with Mr. Klutz before she sat down.

"A.J., we need to talk to you about some-thing," said Mr. Klutz.

Uh-oh. Here it comes.

"I'm sorry I put the worm in Emily's sneaker," I told them.

"You put a worm in Emily's sneaker?!" asked Mr. Klutz.

"Of course not!" I replied. "Whatever gave you *that* idea?"

"A.J., I called you down here because Ms. Coco showed me some of the poems you wrote," Mr. Klutz said. "They are *very* interesting."

"Interesting" is an interesting word. It could mean something is really good, or it could mean something is really bad.

You never know. So if you're not sure if something is good or bad, just say it's interesting.

Ms. Coco handed Mr. Klutz a sheet of paper. He read it out loud.

Tomorrow's Window People
By Arlo Jervis
Someone only fired should soft become hammer.
Imagination!
Because awkward autumn sudden neighbor remain.
Fishhook!
Glow shadow oatmeal tomorrow window people.

When he finished reading, the weirdest thing in the history of the world happened. Mr. Klutz and Ms. Coco started crying! I mean, tears were running down their faces. What a pair of crybabies. They're worse than Emily!

"That's the most beautiful thing I ever heard!" Ms. Coco said.

The two of them were sobbing and blowing their noses into tissues. Well, they blew the *snot* from their noses into the tissues, not the noses themselves. If they blew their noses into tissues, their noses would fall off. That would be weird.

The truth is, I didn't even write that dumb poem. My grandma got me some

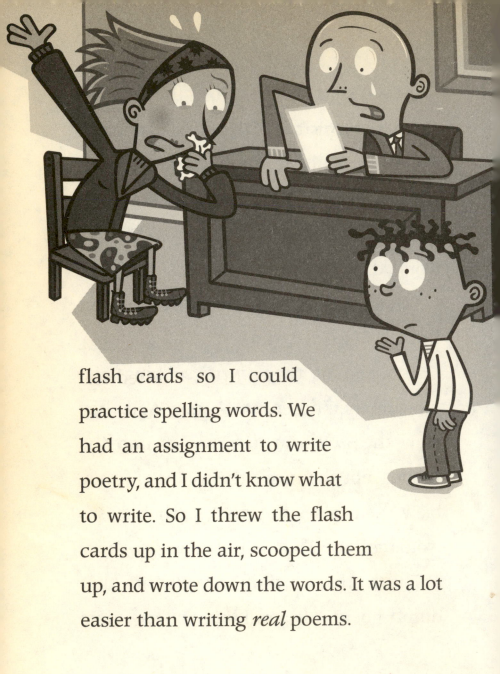

flash cards so I could
practice spelling words. We
had an assignment to write
poetry, and I didn't know what
to write. So I threw the flash
cards up in the air, scooped them
up, and wrote down the words. It was a lot
easier than writing *real* poems.

"We think your poetry is *brilliant*, A.J.," Mr. Klutz said.

"We want to have you tested," said Ms. Coco.

What?! Tested?

"Do I have to pee into a cup?" I asked.

"No, nothing like that," Ms. Coco said. "A.J., we always knew you were gifted. That's why we put you in the gifted and talented program. We want to have you tested to see if you might be a *genius*."

What?! A genius? I'm not a genius! I'm just a regular kid!

"What kind of test are you gonna give me?" I asked.

"Oh, we're not going to give it to you,"

Mr. Klutz said.

"Who will?" I asked.

And you'll never believe who walked into the door at that moment.

Nobody. Because if you walked into a door it would hurt. But you'll never believe who walked into the *doorway*.

It was Dr. Brad, our school counselor!

Dork School

Dr. Brad looks like one of those mad scientists in the movies who straps people to a dentist chair and removes their brain. He's an old guy who wears a bow tie, suspenders, and those weird glasses that only cover one eye. What's up with *that*? And he has crazy hair, like he put his finger

into a lightbulb socket. Somebody should get that guy a comb for his birthday. He is scary looking.

Dr. Brad isn't like a camp counselor. Camp counselors play games, sing songs, and take you on hikes. Dr. Brad is the kind of counselor who just talks to you, which is no fun at all. Talking is boring, especially when you're talking to grown-ups.

Counselors are for kids who are different. Like kids who are smarter or dumber than everybody else. Or kids who learn faster or slower than everybody else. Or kids who have problems. Or kids who don't have problems. Or kids who are left-handed or color-blind. In other words, counselors are for everybody.

"So zees is zee young genius I heard about," Dr. Brad said.

He talks funny.*

Dr. Brad took out a magnifying glass and looked in my eyes. Then he looked

---

*If you read this with a grown-up, ask the grown-up to read Dr. Brad's lines. It will be hilarious.

in my ears. Then he looked in my mouth. Then he looked up my nose.

"You can tell if somebody is a genius by looking at their boogers?" I asked. "That's amazing!"

"Aha-ha-ha-ha," laughed Dr. Brad. "Most amusing."

"What if I *am* a genius?" I asked. "Would that mean I wouldn't have to go to school anymore because I already know everything?"

"No, no, no!" Dr. Brad said. "Zat vould mean vee vould zend you to a special school for genius kids."

"Did you ever hear of Dirk School, A.J.?" asked Ms. Coco.

Dirk School?! Of course I heard of Dirk School. Everybody in our town knows about Dirk School. We call it *Dork* School. It's filled with genius dorks.

"We're afraid that we might be holding you back here at Ella Mentry School," Mr. Klutz told me. "You always say school is boring."

"A.J., you're like a young flower," Ms. Coco said. "If you went to Dirk, they would water you and give you sunshine

to help you grow and bloom."

"I don't want to be a flower!" I yelled. "I don't want to get watered! I want to stay here with my friends! Dork School is filled with dorks! I promise I won't say school is boring anymore. Please don't send me to Dork! Please? Please? Please?"*

"Calm down, A.J.," said Ms. Coco. "Dr. Brad just wants to run a few tests."

---

*If you say "please" enough times, grown-ups will give you whatever you want. That's the first rule of being a kid.

I didn't want to go to Dork School. I decided that nobody would ever think I was a genius. I wouldn't let them.

"I vant to ask a few qvestions, A.J.," Dr. Brad said. "Vut is two plus two?"

"Five," I lied.

"Hmmmmmmm," said Dr. Brad.

Grown-ups always say "hmmmmmmm" when they're thinking. Nobody knows why.

"How vould you spell zee verd 'cat'?" asked Dr. Brad.

"D-O-G," I lied.

"Hmmmmmmm," said Dr. Brad. "Who vas zee first president of zuh United States?"

"A penguin named Binky," I lied.

"*Hmmmmmmm,*" said Dr. Brad.

"What do you think, Doctor?" asked Mr. Klutz.

"Zees young man is a *very* interesting subject," Dr. Brad said.

Uh-oh. He said I was interesting. That could mean *anything*.

"Do you think he might be a genius?" asked Ms. Coco. "The poems he has written are *very* creative."

"I vill need to do furzer tests," Dr. Brad said. "A.J., come vis me to Room 104."

No! Not Room 104!

Room 104 is a mysterious secret room where they put the crazy kids! There are strange sounds and weird machines in there. Everybody says that's where Dr. Brad takes out your brain and puts a monkey brain in its place. When kids go to Room 104, *they never come out again!*

I thought I was gonna die.

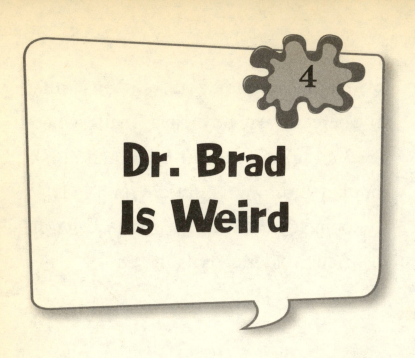

Dr. Brad Is Weird

Dr. Brad gave me a little push into Room 104. There were signs on the walls: **RESPECT OTHERS. BE CONSIDER-ATE. EXPRESS YOUR FEELINGS**. There were a lot of bookshelves, too, some weird-looking machines, and a couch. That's what you lie on when they remove your brain.

Actually, I had been in this room before. One time our security guard, Officer Spence, went crazy and used Dr. Brad's lie detector machine to see if I stole my own peanut butter and jelly sandwich. That was weird.

Officer Spence makes no sense.

"Lie down on zee couch, A.J.," Dr. Brad told me.

"Are you gonna take out my brain and give me a monkey brain?" I asked.

"No, no, no," Dr. Brad said. "I just vant you to look at zeez pictures and tell me vut you see."

I lay on the couch, but I was ready to jump up and run away in case he tried to cut open my skull.

Dr. Brad held a piece of white cardboard in front of me. It looked like somebody spilled ink on it.

"Vut do you see here, A.J.?"

"It looks like somebody spilled some ink on that cardboard," I replied.

"Ees zat all?" Dr. Brad asked. "Don't you see a giant spider who ees jumping on a pogo stick inside a volcano?"

"Uh, no," I said, looking at the card more closely.

Dr. Brad didn't look happy. He took out another card with a different ink blot on it and put it in front of my face.

"And vut do you see here?"

"Looks like another ink blot," I told him.

"Look very closely," Dr. Brad said. "Don't you see a hot dog chasing donuts through a tunnel? Or a big piece of cheese playing Scrabble with two unicorns? Or a man in a red coat eating pistachio nuts in a swimming pool?"

Dr. Brad was getting all excited. His eyebrows were jumping up and down. I looked at the card again.

"Nope," I said. "Looks like an ink blot to me."

"*Hmmm*, interesting," Dr. Brad said as he shook his head and took out another card. "How about zis vun?"

"I guess maybe it looks a little like a cloud," I said, trying to be helpful.

"Don't you see zee umbrella being crushed by zuh hippopotamus? Zee bicycle in zuh sky vis no rider on it? Zee train zat ees being svallowed up by zuh giant boa constrictor?"

"Nope," I said, "I don't see any of those things."

"How can you not see zat?!" Dr. Brad yelled, waving his arms around. "Eet ees so obvious! Are you blind? Eet ees right

zare! Can't you see zee big snake? Vy can't you see zat?"

"I don't know!" I said. "I just don't see it!"

Dr. Brad ripped the last picture into a bunch of little pieces.

"Go back to your class, A.J.," Dr. Brad said. "I vill have to do furzer tests."

I made a dash for the door before he had the chance to change his mind and give me a monkey brain. As I ran down the hall, I could still hear him saying *"Hmmmm, interesting"* over and over again.

The Boys Against the Girls

By the time I got back to Mr. Granite's class, everybody was at lunch. So I went straight to the vomitorium to join the guys. Andrea, Emily, and two of their girl friends were sitting at the next table.

Michael had a bag of Crispy Cheeze-balls. Neil the nude kid had a bag of Cheezy Crispballs. Ryan was eating carrot sticks. Ugh! Ryan will eat *anything*.

"You were in Mr. Klutz's office for a *long* time, A.J.," Michael said. "Did you get in trouble?"

"Yeah, what did he do to you?" asked Neil.

"Are you gonna get kicked out of school?" asked Ryan.

"Nah," I told them, "but Dr. Brad is doing some tests on me. They might send me to Dirk School."

"Dork School?!" the guys yelled.

"Isn't that the school for genius kids?" asked Ryan.

That's when Little Miss Perfect jumped up from her seat.

"What?!" Andrea shouted. *"You're*

35

switching to Dirk?! My mom has been try-ing to get me into Dirk ever since I was in kindergarten! They keep turning me down. If *anybody* should be sent to Dirk School, it's *me*! Not *you*!"

"That's right," said Emily, who always agrees with everything Andrea says.

"I wish you *would* go to Dork School," I told Andrea. "So we wouldn't have you around here anymore."

"Oh, snap!" said Ryan.

"You know, girls are smarter than boys," Andrea said. "Some scientists did an experiment and proved it."

"Some scientists should do an experiment on your *face*," I told Andrea.

"Oh, snap!" said Ryan.

"You're mean, A.J.!" Emily said.

"She started it," I said.

"Boys eat mud!" said Andrea's other

little flunky, who was named Annette.

"Girls have six toes on each foot!" said Neil the nude kid. I knew that wasn't true, but it sounded good.

"Boys are smelly!" said Julie, who was also sitting at Andrea's table.

"Boys go to college to get more knowledge!" said Michael. "Girls go to Jupiter to get more stupider!"

Everybody was yelling at one another. Kids at the other tables were looking at us. I was trying to think of something really mean to say about girls, but I couldn't come up with anything good. It didn't matter though, because at that moment, Dr. Brad came rushing over to our table.

"SHTOP!" he hollered. Everybody shtopped, I mean, stopped.

It was so quiet, you could hear a pin drop. Not a bowling pin, though. They make a lot of noise when they drop. I mean one of those little pins, like the ones my mom uses to sew stuff.

"No more of zees fighting!" Dr. Brad yelled. "No more shouting! You must learn to get along!"

Dr. Brad went on and on, telling us that boys and girls need to be polite and respectful of one another so we can live in peace and harmony and all that other stuff counselors always say.

Everybody was quiet while he talked. We all looked at the floor. Any time a grown-up yells, you're supposed to look at the floor. Nobody knows why.

"I'm sorry, Dr. Brad," said Andrea, who never misses the chance to brownnose a grown-up.

"Are we going to be punished?" asked Emily quietly.

"No, no, no," Dr. Brad said. "I have anuzer idea. Tomorrow morning, I vant each of you to bring in your favorite toy from home."

"What?" I asked. "Our favorite toy?"

"Zat's right," Dr. Brad said. "Come to Room 104 vis your toy first zing in zee morning."

"But—" Ryan said.

"NO BUTS!" shouted Dr. Brad.

We all giggled because Dr. Brad said "but," which sounds the same as "butt" even if it's spelled differently.* Any time a grown-up says "but," you should giggle. That's the first rule of being a kid.

---

*Just like "duty" and "doody." It's impossible to hear the word "duty" and not think of "doody."

6

The War to End All Wars

The next morning, I brought Striker Smith to school with me. He's a superhero action figure from the future who travels through time and fights bad guys with a sword that's attached to his hand. Striker Smith is cool. He can turn into a jet plane and fly, too.

One time on
the school bus
I tied a string to
Striker Smith's
leg and threw
him out the
window so
he could fight
bad guys who
were attacking
the bus. But Striker
fell under the bus and got decapitated.
That's a fancy way of saying his head came
off. I was really sad. The good news is that
I got a *new* Striker Smith for Christmas.

Michael brought in a Chewbacca action

figure from *Star Wars*. Ryan brought in Megatron, who is a Transformer who fights in the epic battle between the Autobots and Decepticons. Neil the nude kid brought in Private Gunn, who is a helicopter assault trooper who can breathe underwater. He comes with an attack dog and a deluxe blowtorch.

Action figures are cool.

The girls, of course, brought in their Barbies.

"This is Ballerina Barbie," Andrea said when we all met outside Room 104. "Isn't she lovely?"

"Oh yes!" said Emily. "Do you like my Circus Star Barbie?"

"I brought in Ponytail Barbie," said Annette.

"I brought in Wedding Barbie," said Julie.

Ugh. Just listening to girls talk about Barbies made me want to throw up. But soon Dr. Brad arrived. He unlocked the door and let us into his office.

"Zeez are very nice toys you have," he told us.

"Why did you tell us to bring them to school?" asked Andrea.

"I vant you to trade toys vis each uhzer," he said.

Huh?

"I vant each boy to geeve your favorite

toy to a girl," said Dr. Brad, "and each girl to geeve your favorite toy to a boy."

"What?!" I said. "I'm not giving a girl my Striker Smith!"

"Zees vill help each of you relate to others," Dr. Brad said. "Geeve it a try, A.J. Just for a few minutes."

"Here, Arlo," Andrea said, "you can play with my Barbie."

Andrea held out her Barbie to me. I backed away like she was holding up a dead rat. I didn't want to touch the thing.

"Ugh!" I shouted. "Barbie germs!"

"Don't be silly," Dr. Brad said. "Zees vill be fun!"

He took our action figures and gave them to the girls. He took the Barbies and gave one to each of us guys.

"I'm not playing with a *doll*," I announced.

"You already *do*, Arlo," said Andrea. "Action figures are just dolls for boys."

"They are not," I said.

"Are too."

We went back and forth like that for a while until I finally had to say "R2D2." Any time somebody says "are too," you should say "R2D2." That's the first rule of being a kid.

"You better not break our action figures!" Ryan warned the girls.

"You better not break our Barbies!" said Andrea.

"SHTOP!" shouted Dr. Brad.

He led me and the guys across the hall to the conference room. Dr. Brad told us to play with the Barbies and he would come and check up on us in a little while. Then he left and closed the door behind him.

I looked at Michael. Michael looked at Neil. Neil looked at Ryan. Ryan looked at me. I looked at Barbie.

"I don't want to play with Barbies," said Neil the nude kid.

"Me neither," said Michael.

"Hey," I said, "I have an idea! Let's have a Barbie war!"

"A.J., you're a genius!" said Michael. "No wonder they want to send you to Dork School."

Me and Michael put two Barbies on one

end of the long table. Ryan and Neil put the other two Barbies at the far end.

It was time for *war*! The war to end all wars. The War of the Barbies!

There was just one problem. Barbies don't come with weapons or anything cool that shoots. What fun are toys if they can't shoot anything?

But that's when I came up with the genius idea of the century. There was a box of rubber bands on the windowsill. I gave a handful of them to Neil, Ryan, and Michael.

The guys said I should get the No Bell Prize. That's a prize they give out to people who don't have bells.

"Ready! Aim! FIRE!" I yelled.

It was all-out war! Me and Michael and Ryan and Neil were going crazy. The air was thick with flying rubber bands.

"Die, Ballerina Barbie!" I shouted.

"Eat lead, Circus Star Barbie!" shouted Ryan.

"Ooooh! My Barbie has been hit!" shouted Neil.

"We might have to amputate her head to save her life!" shouted Michael.

Rubber bands were flying fast and furious when the most amazing thing in the history of the world happened.

The door opened.

Well, that's not the amazing part, because doors open all the time. That's what they do. They're *doors*. But suddenly, Dr. Brad burst in.

"Vut's going on in here?" he shouted. "I heard a lot of noise."

"We're fighting the ultimate battle of good versus evil," I explained, "with Barbies."

"Shtop it!" yelled Dr. Brad. "No more fighting!"

Dr. Brad was really mad. He made us pick up all the rubber bands.

"We're sorry," Ryan said.

"I hope zee girls did not treat your action figures zuh same vay you treated their dolls!" Dr. Brad said as he led us back across the hall to Room 104.

And you'll never believe in a million hundred years what we saw in Room 104.

Chewbacca was wearing a dress! He was holding a little purse and posed next to a little ironing board!

Private Gunn had a wig on his head, a little hair dryer in his hand, and pink ice skates on his feet!

Megatron had on a tutu, and wore

bracelets on his arms!

And Striker Smith was wearing high heels!

"What did you do to our action figures?!" I shouted at the girls.

"We're playing dress up," said Annette.

"Doesn't Striker Smith look adorable in turquoise heels?" asked Emily.

"We accessorized him!" said Andrea.

Ahhhhhhhhhhhhhhhhhhhhhhhhhhhhhh!!!!

Love and Hate

Dr. Brad wasn't very happy with the results of his toy-swapping experiment. When he asked if we learned anything from it, I said, "Barbies would be a lot less lame if they came with weapons."

So I knew I was in trouble when we were back in class and an announcement came over the loudspeaker.

"Mr. Granite, please send A.J. to Room 104."

"*Ooooooooooooooooooooooooh!*" everybody oooooohed.

"He's probably gonna give you electric shocks," Michael whispered to me. "I saw that in a movie once. Some doctor held these paddles against a guy's head and shot a million volts of electricity through his brain. It was cool."

I walked *really* slowly down the hall to Room 104. I didn't want Dr. Brad to hold paddles against my head and give me electric shocks.

Well, when I got to Room 104, you'll never believe in a million hundred years what Dr. Brad had on his desk.

Paddles!

"Are you going to give me electric shocks?" I said, trembling with fear.

"No, no, no," he replied. "Mr. Klutz asked me to play Ping-Pong vis him. He says it's a great way to get rid of stress."

Whew!

Dr. Brad told me to lie on the couch.

"Are you going to give me a monkey brain?" I asked.

"No, no, no!" he said. "Vee are going to play a leetle game. I vant you to close your eyes, A.J. Ven I say a verd, I vant you to say zee first verd zat comes into your mind. Okay?"

"Okay," I said, closing my eyes.

Dr. Brad: "Fast"

Me: "Slow"

Dr. Brad: "Up"

Me: "Down"

Dr. Brad: "Skinny"

Me: "Fat"

Dr. Brad: "Bad"

Me: "Good"

Dr. Brad: "Hard"

Me: "Soft"

Dr. Brad: "Love"

Me: "Andrea—I mean, hate"

"Aha!" said Dr. Brad.

"What?" I said, opening my eyes. "What did I do?"

"You said 'Andrea'!"

"So?" I asked.

"Before zat moment, you vere saying opposites to every verd, A.J. Zen, ven I said 'love,' you said 'Andrea.'"

"Well," I explained, "that's because I hate Andrea. And hate is the opposite of love, so Andrea is the opposite of love."

"If hate is zee opposite of love, vy didn't you just say 'hate' *first*?" asked Dr. Brad.

"I don't know," I said. "It just came out."

Dr. Brad leaned over and stuck his face close to mine.

"A.J.," he said, "are you in love vis Andrea?"

"No!" I said. "I already told you! I *hate* Andrea! That's why I said the word

'Andrea' when you said 'love'!"

"Maybe you just *say* you hate Andrea to hide zee fact zat you really *love* Andrea. *Hmmmmmm?* Isn't zat possible, A.J.? Boys sometimes tease girls zay like. Perhaps if you vould simply admit zat you really deep down

inside love Andrea, zee two of you could get along better. No?"

"No!" I shouted. "It's not true! I don't love Andrea! Why are you asking me these questions? I thought you just wanted to find out if I was a genius."

"A.J.," he said, leaning his face even closer to me, "I zink zat now vee are getting somevere."

Take Me to Your Leader

I *don't* love Andrea! I don't, don't, don't, don't, don't, don't, don't, don't, don't, don't, don't, don't, don't, don't, don't, don't!

Boy, when you say the word "don't" over and over again, it really sounds weird.

Dr. Brad took a shiny metal thing out of his desk drawer. It was attached to a string,

61

and he dangled it in front of my face. He began swinging it back and forth.

"A.J.," Dr. Brad said, "I vant you to look at zees very closely."

"Why?" I asked.

"Do you know vut hypnosis ees?" asked Dr. Brad.

Sure I knew what hypnosis was. I saw it on TV once. This hypnotist guy had some lady stare at a shiny watch, and he put her in a trance. Then he made her dance around like a chicken, and everybody laughed.

"Are you gonna hypnotize me?" I asked.

"Isn't zees shiny?" Dr. Brad said. "Stare at it as it svings back and forth. Your eyelids are feeling a leetle heavy, no?"

"Heavy . . ." I mumbled.

"Stare at zee shiny object as it svings back and forth . . . back and forth . . . back and forth," said Dr. Brad. "You are feeling sleepy, A.J., no?"

"Sleepy . . ." I mumbled.

"Stare at zee shiny object as it svings back and forth . . . back and forth . . . back

and forth," said Dr. Brad. "Soon you vill be in a hypnotic trance."

"Trance . . ." I mumbled.

"You vill do everyzing I say," said Dr. Brad.

"Everything you say . . ." I mumbled.

"And ven I snap my fingers, you vill vake up," said Dr. Brad.

"Wake up," I mumbled.

The truth is, I was totally yanking Dr. Brad's chain. I wasn't in a trance. I wasn't hypnotized for a second. I was just playing along.

"I am from the planet Zorg," I said in my best robot voice. "Take me to your leader."

Then I got up off the couch and danced

around like a chicken.

"Most amusing, A.J.," said Dr. Brad. "I knew you vere not in a trance all along."

"How did you know?" I asked.

"Eet ees very hard to hypnotize geniuses," Dr. Brad said.

"Oh no!" I said. "Does this mean I'm a genius? Are you gonna send me to Dork School?"

"Time vill tell," he replied. "I vill complete my report at zee end of zuh day. You vill know first zing in zee morning. You can go back to class now."

The Greatest Moment of My Life

By the time Dr. Brad let me go, it was afternoon recess. I ran over to join the guys on the playground.

"So, did Dr. Brad give you electric shocks?" asked Michael.

"Did he take out your brain?" asked Ryan.

"Nah," I told them, "he tried to hypnotize me, but it didn't work. Hypnosis is way overrated. Dr. Brad said that geniuses are really hard to hypnotize."

Andrea and her girly friends were listening to us, as usual.

"I bet it would be *really* hard to hypnotize *me* then," said Andrea.

"Oh, I could probably hypnotize you in a minute," I told Andrea.

"Could not!"

"Could too!"

We went back and forth like that for a while. Finally, Andrea dared me to try and hypnotize her. I told her I would need a shiny object, so she took off her necklace and handed it to me.

"This is really shiny," I said. "Stare at it as it swings back and forth."

"Okay," Andrea said.

I swung the necklace in front of Andrea's face.

"Are your eyelids feeling heavy?" I asked.

"Heavy . . ." Andrea mumbled.

"Stare at the necklace as it swings back and forth . . . back and forth . . . back and forth," I told Andrea. "Are you feeling sleepy?"

"Sleepy . . ." she mumbled.

"Stare at the shiny necklace as it swings back and forth . . . back and forth . . . back and forth," I told Andrea. "Soon you'll be in a trance."

"Trance . . ." she mumbled.

"Hey, I think it's working," Michael said. "Look at her eyes. She's in a trance!"

"No she's not," I said. "She's just faking it. That's what I did."

"I don't like this, A.J.," said Emily. She looked like she was going to cry, like always.

"You will do everything I say," I told Andrea. "You will believe everything I say."

"Everything you say . . ." Andrea mumbled like a robot.

"You will listen only to me," I told Andrea.

"Only to you . . ." she mumbled.

"And when I snap my fingers, you'll wake up," I told Andrea.

"Wake up," she mumbled.

"A.J., you're gonna get in trouble," Ryan said. "She's like, in another world."

"Relax," I whispered. "I'm just having a little fun."

"It doesn't look like fun to *me*," whined Emily.

"You will believe anything I say," I told Andrea.

"Anything you say . . ." she mumbled.

"You're a big dumbhead," I told Andrea.

"I'm a big dumbhead . . ." she mumbled.

"Oh, snap!" said Ryan. "She's *gotta* be in a trance if she would say *that*!"

"That's mean!" Emily said. "Wake her up, A.J.!"

"You hate school," I told Andrea.

"Hate school . . ." she mumbled.

"Following rules is for losers," I told Andrea.

"Following rules is for losers," she mumbled. This was fun!

"You're a bad kid," I told Andrea.

"I'm a bad kid . . ." mumbled Andrea.

Making Andrea say she was bad was hilarious. This was the greatest moment of my life.

"Your feet smell like rotten cabbage," I told Andrea.

"Stop fooling around, A.J.!" Neil said. "It's almost time to go back inside. You better wake her up before the bell rings."

"Okay, okay," I said. "When I snap my fingers, Andrea, you will wake up."

But I didn't get the chance to snap my fingers, because at that very moment . . .

BRRRRING! BRRRRING!

Recess was over.

Little Miss Not-So-Perfect

10

When the bell rang, we all ran inside the school. Andrea looked like everything was normal.

But I knew something was wrong. When she went running inside, Andrea didn't even ask for her necklace back. I put it in my pocket.

And she wasn't acting normal either. As soon as we got into Mr. Granite's class, Little Miss Perfect put her feet up on her desk, leaned back in her chair, and put both of her hands behind her head. Andrea *never* sits that way. She always sits with her hands folded and her feet on the floor.

"Andrea," said Mr. Granite, "sit correctly, please."

"Make me," Andrea replied.*

Well, everybody's jaws dropped open. Andrea *never* says "Make me."

---

*That's what you say when you really want to be obnoxious. *Make me.* Anybody who says "Make me" is asking for trouble.

"I beg your pardon, Andrea?" asked Mr. Granite.

"I said, Make me!" Andrea shouted. "Why don't you clean the dirt out of your ears so you can hear?"

"Ooooooooooooooooooooooooh!" everybody oooooohed.

"Oh, snap!" said Ryan.

I couldn't believe what I was hearing! Andrea is usually such a big brownnoser.

She *never* talks back to grown-ups.

"Are you feeling okay, Andrea?" asked Mr. Granite. "Do you know who you are?"

"My name is Andrea, and I hate school," Andrea said. "Following rules is for losers."

"Maybe you want to go see Mrs. Cooney, the school nurse," said Mr. Granite. "Maybe you need to lie down."

"Maybe you need to shut your face!" said Andrea.

"Oooooooooooooooooooooooh!" everybody ooooohed.

"She's in a trance!" Emily shouted. "A.J. hypnotized her on the playground. And now she thinks she's a mean kid!"

"You should shut your face, too," Andrea told Emily. "You're an annoying little crybaby."

"Ooooooooooooooooooooooooh!" everybody oooooohed.

Andrea suddenly got up, knocking her chair over. "I've had enough of this dump," she said. "I'm outta here!" Then she stormed out the door.

It was the most amazing thing in the history of the world! And we got to see it live and in person. You should have been there!

But what happened next was even *more* amazing. A few seconds after Andrea stormed out of the classroom . . .

BRRRRING! BRRRRING!

"Oh no!" Mr. Granite said. "What a terrible time for a fire drill."

"It's not a fire drill!" Ryan shouted. "I think Andrea pulled the fire alarm in the hall!"

"We have to leave the building," Mr. Granite announced. "Everybody line up in single file. Michael, you're the door holder. Emily, you're the line leader."

We all lined up and started filing out of the room. The other classes were in the hallway, too.

"A.J., you've got to stop Andrea!" Michael whispered as we marched out of the building. "You're the one who hypnotized her."

"What do you want *me* to do?" I asked.

"You just have to snap your fingers and she'll come out of the trance," Neil the nude kid said.

Neil was right. Me and the guys rushed out onto the playground. The whole school was there. I looked all around for Andrea so I could snap my fingers and bring her out of the trance.

But she was gone.

A Very Dangerous Situation

Mr. Klutz and our vice principal, Mrs. Jafee, came running out onto the playground. They were followed by Dr. Brad, who was huffing and puffing.

"Vut's going on?" Dr. Brad shouted.

"Somebody pulled the fire alarm, by golly!" said Mrs. Jafee.

"It was Andrea Young," Mr. Granite said.

"Are you sure?" asked Mr. Klutz. "That's not the Andrea *I* know. I'm sure Dr. Brad will be able to calm her down."

"Vere is Andrea?" asked Dr. Brad. "I must speak vis her."

"We don't know where she is," I told them. "She ran out of the school. She could be anywhere."

At that moment, the strangest thing in the history of the world happened. We heard a voice from above our heads.

"I'm up here, you dumbheads!"

I looked up. And there, standing on the roof of the school, was Andrea!

"WOW!" everybody said, which is

"MOM" upside down.

It was a real Kodak moment. Kids started pointing at Andrea and yelling.

"She's crazy!" "She's nuts!" "She's loopy!" "She's bananas!" "She's off the wall!" "She's out of her mind!" "She's loony!" "She's bizarre!" "She's off her rocker!" "She's not normal!" "She's loco!" "She's bonkers!" "She's losing her marbles!" "She's screwy!" "She's out of control!"

"How did you get up there, Andrea?" shouted Mr. Klutz.

"How do you *think* I got up here, you big doofus?" yelled Andrea. "I climbed."

"Ooooooooooooooooooooooh!" everybody ooooooohed.

I couldn't believe Andrea called the principal a big doofus!

"My feet smell like rotten cabbage!" Andrea yelled.

I snapped my fingers to make Andrea come out of her trance. But she was too far away to hear.

"What should we do, Dr. Brad?" asked Mr. Klutz. "You're the school counselor!"

"Zees ees a very dangerous situation," Dr. Brad said. "I must talk to Andrea and show her kindness, caring, and understanding."

"That won't do anything!" Michael said. "A.J. hypnotized her. She's only going to listen to him."

"Ees zees true, A.J.?" asked Dr. Brad.

"You hypnotized Andrea?"

I didn't have the chance to answer his question, because at that moment a bunch of fire engines and police cars pulled up to the school with their sirens screaming. Somebody must have called 911!

A policeman with a bullhorn got out of one of the cars.

"Get down from there, young lady!" he shouted.

"Come and get me, coppers!" yelled Andrea.

"We don't want you to get hurt," another policeman shouted.

"You'll never take me alive!" yelled Andrea. She picked up a tennis ball off the roof and threw it at the police car.

"Let's get her, men!" the cop with the bullhorn shouted. The cops started moving toward the wall.

"Vait!" Dr. Brad shouted. "Zees ees a very dangerous situation! Do not go up on zee roof. Zare ees only vun person here who can rescue zees girl."

Dr. Brad looked at me. Mr. Klutz looked at me. Mrs. Jafee looked at me. The cops looked at me. *Everybody* was looking at me!

I was faced with the hardest decision of my life. If I didn't save Andrea, something horrible might happen. And if I did save Andrea, the guys would say I was in love with her. I was thinking so hard that my brain hurt.

I didn't know what to say. I didn't know what to do. I had to think fast.

"I'm going up," I said.

Everybody cheered as I dug my sneaker into the little space between the bricks. There were a few windowsills I could step on, too. It was hard, but soon I reached the top of the school. I was a few feet from Andrea.

"Get out of my face, A.J.!" she yelled.

I took Andrea's necklace out of my pocket and

dangled it in front of her eyes. She stared at it.

"You will do everything I say," I told her.

"Everything you say . . ." Andrea mumbled.

"You're a *good* girl," I said. "You never do anything wrong. You love school and books and learning and being nice to grown-ups. When I snap my fingers, you'll wake up and go back to the way you used to be."

"The way I used to be . . ." mumbled Andrea.

SNAP!

Andrea was startled. She looked at me like she was seeing me for the first time. Then she looked around.

"What am I doing up here on the roof,

Arlo?" she asked.

"You . . . uh, went a little crazy," I told her. "Let's climb back down now, okay?"

"Okay," said Andrea.

Me and Andrea carefully climbed back down the wall of the school. When we reached the ground, everybody cheered. Andrea gave me a big hug.

"You saved my life, Arlo!" she said.

"Oooooh!" Ryan said. "A.J. saved Andrea's life. "They must be in *love*!"

"When are you gonna get married?" asked Michael.

If those guys weren't my best friends, I would hate them.

The Moment of Truth

12

As soon as I got to Mr. Granite's class the next morning, there was an announcement over the loudspeaker.

"Please send A.J. to Mr. Klutz's office."

Everybody looked at me. We all knew what was about to happen. I was going to find out whether or not they would send me to Dork School. Everybody got up to shake my hand, even Mr. Granite.

"It's been nice knowing you, A.J.," said Ryan.

"Good luck, dude," Michael said. "I hope we'll still be friends."

"We'll miss you," said Neil the nude kid.

Andrea came over. I thought she was going to hug me or kiss me or do some other disgusting thing.

"I've been thinking about it, Arlo," Andrea said. "Maybe it would be *good* if you went to Dirk. It might be better for both of us if we went to different schools."

"Yeah, maybe you're right," I agreed.

I walked down the hall more slowly than I had ever walked down any hall. A glacier could have beat me to Mr. Klutz's office.* But finally, I got there. It was the moment of truth.

I put my hand on the doorknob.

I turned the doorknob.

I opened the door.

And you'll never believe in a million hundred years who was sitting there.

It was Dr. Brad. And he was crying. Big tears were rolling down his face.

"It vuz all my fault," he blubbered. "If Andrea had fallen off the roof, I don't know vut I vould have done."

---

*That is, if there were glaciers inside schools.

"There, there," said Mr. Klutz and Ms. Coco as they patted Dr. Brad on his back. "Everything turned out fine."

They were trying to comfort him, but it was no use. Dr. Brad fell to the floor and started weeping like a baby.

"Wahhhhhhhhhhhhhh!"

Sheesh, get a grip!

"Dr. Brad has gone mad," Ms. Coco told me. "We don't know what to do."

"We thought you might be able to help, A.J.," said Mr. Klutz. "You seem to be good at this sort of thing."

"Maybe Dr. Brad isn't a counselor at all," I told them. "Did you ever think of that? Maybe he kidnapped our real counselor and stuffed him in the trunk of his car. Stuff like that happens all the time, you know."

"I don't think that's it, A.J.," said Mr. Klutz.

I tried really hard to think of a way to make Dr. Brad snap out of it. I thought so hard I was afraid my head was gonna explode. And then I came up with the greatest idea in the history of the world.

"We must resort to drastic measures!" I shouted.

I rushed out of Mr. Klutz's office and ran down the hall to Room 104. The Ping-Pong paddles were still on Dr. Brad's desk. I scooped them up and ran back to Mr. Klutz's office. Dr. Brad was still on the floor, freaking out.

"Are you going to give me electric shocks?" he asked.

"No, no, no," I told him. "We're gonna play Ping-Pong!"

We helped Dr. Brad up and gave him a

paddle. Mr. Klutz and Ms. Coco picked up paddles and went to the other side of the table.

"Volley for serve," I said.

I hit the ball to Mr. Klutz. Mr. Klutz hit the ball to Dr. Brad. Dr. Brad hit the ball to Ms. Coco. Ms. Coco hit the ball to me.

"I feel better already!" said Dr. Brad.

"Ping-Pong is great for getting rid of stress," said Mr. Klutz.

The four of us had a blast! Instead of learning boring stuff like math, science, and social studies, I got to play Ping-Pong all morning with Dr. Brad, Mr. Klutz, and Ms. Coco. It was the greatest day of my life!

Well, that's pretty much what happened. Maybe Dr. Brad will get better. Maybe he'll comb his hair and stop looking up my nose with a magnifying glass. Maybe he'll remove my brain and replace it with a monkey brain. Maybe I'll have to pee into a cup and they'll send me to Dork School. Maybe I'll cut down a tree so I can make a reading log. Maybe Ms. Coco will stop crying over my lame poems and saying I'm a genius. Maybe Andrea will go crazy again and climb up on the roof. Maybe the girls will stop accessorizing our action figures. Maybe me and the guys will have another War of the Barbies. Maybe the boys and girls at Ella Mentry School will learn to stop fighting, respect one another, and live in peace and harmony.

But it won't be easy!

Check out the My Weird School series!

#1: Miss Daisy Is Crazy!
The first book in the hilarious series stars A.J., a second grader who hates school—and can't believe his teacher hates it too!

#2: Mr. Klutz Is Nuts!
A.J. can't believe his crazy principal wants to climb to the top of the flagpole!

#3: Mrs. Roopy Is Loopy!
The new librarian thinks she's George Washington one day and Little Bo Peep the next!

#4: Ms. Hannah Is Bananas!
The art teacher wears clothes made from pot holders. Worse than that, she's trying to make A.J. be partners with yucky Andrea!

#5: Miss Small Is off the Wall!
The gym teacher is teaching A.J.'s class to juggle scarves, balance feathers, and do everything *but* play sports!

#6: Mr. Hynde Is Out of His Mind!
The music teacher plays bongo drums on the principal's bald head! But does he have what it takes to be a real rock-and-roll star?

#7: Mrs. Cooney Is Loony!
The school nurse is everybody's favorite—but is she hiding a secret identity?

#8: Ms. LaGrange Is Strange!
The new lunch lady talks funny—and why is she writing secret messages in the mashed potatoes?

#9: Miss Lazar Is Bizarre!
What kind of grown-up *likes* cleaning throw-up? Miss Lazar is the weirdest custodian in the world!

#10: Mr. Docker Is off His Rocker!
The science teacher alarms and amuses A.J.'s class with his wacky experiments and nutty inventions.

#11: Mrs. Kormel Is Not Normal!
A.J.'s school bus gets a flat tire, then becomes hopelessly lost at the hands of the wacky bus driver.

#12: Ms. Todd Is Odd!
Ms. Todd is subbing, and A.J. and his friends are sure she kidnapped Miss Daisy so she could take over her job.

#13: Mrs. Patty Is Batty!
A little bit of spookiness and a lot of humor add up to the best trick-or-treating adventure ever!

#14: Miss Holly Is Too Jolly!
Mistletoe means kissletoe, the worst tradition in the history of the world!

#15: Mr. Macky Is Wacky!
Mr. Macky expects A.J. and his friends to read stuff about the presidents…and even dress up like them! He's taking Presidents' Day way too far!

#16: Ms. Coco Is Loco!
It's Poetry Month and the whole school is poetry crazy, thanks to Ms. Coco. She talks in rhyme! She thinks boys should have feelings! Is she crazy?

#17: Miss Suki Is Kooky!
Miss Suki is a very famous author who writes about ndangered animals. But when her pet raptor gets loose during a school visit, it's the kids who are endangered!

#18: Mrs. Yonkers Is Bonkers!
Mrs. Yonkers builds a robot substitute teacher to take her place for a day!

#19: Dr. Carbles Is Losing His Marbles!
Dr. Carbles, the president of the board of education, is fed up with Mr. Klutz and wants to fire him. Will A.J. and his friends be able to save their principal's job?

#20: Mr. Louie Is Screwy!
When the hippie crossing guard, Mr. Louie, puts a love potion in the water fountain, everyone at Ella Mentry School falls in love!

#21: Ms. Krup Cracks Me Up!
A.J. thinks that nothing can possibly be as boring as a sleepover in the natural history museum. But anything can happen when Ms. Krup is in charge.